Poems

Chosen

In the evening, I contemplate.
I feel I should go out for a run.
I must move quickly if I'm to make it.
Before too long, there will be no more sun.

I drive far and away from my residence
I park in the middle of nowhere.
I spot a path heading into the woods.
I think to myself, "no one would ever go there."

I warm my muscles for a few minutes.
Afterwards, I begin to jog.
The trail started as clear as clean water,
But ahead of me there's fog.

I've run good distance.
I covered a ton of ground
I'm close to exhaustion.
It's probably time I turned around

Before I turned, I see a house in the distance
While I would normally move along,
My curiosity this time was persistent.

As I walked closer and closer,

I analyzed the scene.
Approximately 20 feet away, my body started to
lean.

I turned around and tried to run in the opposite
direction
My feet were moving but I wasn't going anywhere.
It denied my attempted ejection.

By some sort of mysterious force,
I was sucked to into the house.
I assumed it was empty but what appeared through
the smoke and the fog was a woman in a black
blouse.

I say to her, "why have you brought me here? What
do you want from me?"
She quickly responded, "You better speak to me
carefully, for I have powers you wouldn't believe."

"If you must know why,
You're here because I'm in need.
I have a duty to fulfill.
You're here to execute this deed."

With concern in my voice I said, "I don't want to
carry out any deeds for you. I have my own life. I
have my goals."

With a stern voice she said, "That's too bad. You no longer have a choice. You will do what your told!"

Before I could respond I was slammed on the ground and rendered immobile.
She didn't even need to touch me. As crazy as that sounds, she drew a line around me in the shape of an oval.

She placed red colored liquid on my forehead and told me to be still.
She whispered in my ear, "This'll hurt pretty bad, but you won't be killed."
I said, "After this procedure, will I be healed." She responded confidently, "Yes, but only after you've used your new skills."

She put her hands on my head.
All I can see is huge, bright light beam,
The pain was excruciating.
It was extreme. Although I tried my hardest, I couldn't scream.
The next thing I remember, I woke up in my bed.
My mind or reality I could not deem.
I sat up and asked myself, "Did that really just happen or was it all a dream?"

Spirit of The Moon

Moon spirit I can see who you truly are
I know that you're misunderstood.
You heart is filled with nothing but love.
Give your all for them, I know you would.
You spend your time protecting the innocent.
They owe you much than they should.
Your light is too bright. They can't fathom it. No
matter how much I wish that they could.

We held each other's hand in a previous life, I'd
say you and I are destiny.
From perfection I slipped. Time away we've spent.
I can't help but to feel jealousy.
I failed to resist the seduction of Mars, but that
didn't make you think any less of me.
Even in times when I felt trapped,
You spoke your words so heavenly.

The luminous bodies behind you,
Are the ones you love the most.
Even at the at the apogee of your evolution, you'd
prefer to keep them close.
I hardly see them when you are near.
You stand in front of ghosts.
The kingdom is where our future awaits.
I'll have them prepare their queen a toast.

*The night is young, and you're surprised when a
villain approached your team.
They researched and found your weakness. This
took time to scheme.
Not too long ago, I had a vision.
My powers enable my dreams.
When hope seems lost and you're in need, I
guarantee you'll hear my theme.*

*I'll be there for you no matter what.
It is your love that I am proposed.
Lonely is what you'll never feel again.
From this day forward, our souls are juxtaposed.
The evil you fight so selflessly, will try to keep you
enclosed.
Not even past my dying breath, will I ever leave
you with woes.
Now my love, calm yourself.
Open your eyes. What you find should leave you
composed.
The darkness was defeated...
Off to the side, you'll see my rose.*

Spontaneous Combustion

*There once was ice, but now there's fire.
I'm reaching for your deepest desire.
I'm always alert, I never get tired.
I'm levitating now, but I'm going higher.*

My eyes have changed, they're glowing red
I'm doing the things that I once said.
Don't want to see my people misled.
I'd rather see them flourish instead.

My hands have switched. They now shoot rockets.
They put the green stuff in your pockets.
That glass will break if you don't watch it.
It feels amazing. So, I won't stop it.

Jump on the ride. I heard it lifts.
I'm taking advantage of this gift.
Push down the clutch, before you shift.
Now move along and make it swift.

The sense I have leaves a concern.
I can't sit still. My spirit has burned.
Expand the mind. Increase what you've learned.
I'll give to you the thing you've yearned.

I'm about to break Da Vinci's code.
I'm about to receive what I'm owed.
The chains halted what was bestowed.
Now that they're gone watch me explode!

Unprecedented Impression

Curious is my current sentiment but

I can't place my finger on it.
A glow that comes around once a millennium,
Just like the rarest of comets.
Any outfit you seem to wear,
transforms when you decide to don it.
You helped me realize I had a real talent,
When you inspired my first sonnet.

I don't know you very well.
In fact, I don't know you at all.
I have no idea how you've made this impression.
No estimations of what would befall.
I can't begin to explain this feeling.
I don't think I could even recall.
I glanced past what was physical,
And what I saw has me enthralled.

I assume you observe with different lenses.
You carry yourself with decency.
When I told you before, (You probably thought I
was joking)
I think we occupy the same frequency.
How do you make it look so simple?
You shine your grace so easily.
I hope these words caress your ears.
To that I'll respond gleefully.

This is new territory for me.
I'm a foreigner in this land.

I'm not sure how to react.
What do I do with my hands?
You're remarkably sturdy as I expected.
I know there's a lot that you withstand.
"A Passion for Elegance" may not have piqued
your interest.
It's time for the next step in the plan.

I know the difficulties of the path 7 well.
Most people will fail to comprehend.
With hearts that reach passion at the highest of
levels.
A mind that continually transcends.
We must be careful with our energy.
There's only so much we can expend.
Only a few will ever infiltrate our lives.
Even less in which we'll depend.

I'm looking for kindred spirits.
Individuals in which I share a relation.
On my quest for knowledge and constant
improvement,
You could galvanize my mentation.
If this piece of mine fails to manifest,
I'll write a song and try serenation.
All I ask is that you oblige me,
With a single conversation.

Break the Cycle

A long while I've stayed silent.
I was afraid of judgments.
I no longer suffer from that disease
I think it's time we discussed it.

If there are issues you can see,
Patterns to disallow.
Don't wait for the beginning of a new year.
The time to change is now.

You were born into a racist family
That's highly unfortunate.
You have your own eyes
No need to be proportionate.

Your parents were addicts.
As a child, drugs were all around you.
There are other ways to find happiness.
The answers are within. You will find the truth

You grew up in poverty.
You've had to fight and sweat for everything.
I know you're sometimes tempted seeing others.
Educate yourself. You can't imagine the
opportunities it'll bring.

Happiness is foreign in your household.
You're in the midst of a trial.

Absorb as much positivity possible.
When your goals are reached it'll be worthwhile.

You dislike yourself at the moment.
All you can see is flaws.
After all that you've been through,
You deserve a round of applause.

Here's something I'm particularly passionate
about.
I huge problem in our world today
It's not uplifting but this is a message I must relay.
I know you want a family.
I know you have pressure.
I know you want to please your ancestors.
However, please don't bring a child into this
weather If you're struggling with your own
endeavors.
Our children deserve better.
So please!! Don't add another life to treasure if
you don't yet have yourself together.
Don't let the cycle continue forever when you know
it needs to be severed.

Lost Love Lessons Learned

You're such a joyous person.
You were always full of smiles.
Your love for me was unmatched.

I believe it'll stay that way for a while.
It's a shame you caught me during my most
ignorant chapter.
I enjoyed our time together and even though it was
short it was full of fun and laughter.

You were the first I ever loved. It's strange
because we
were very different.
Constant communication made us grow extremely
close.
We had a rare bond. When I spoke, you always
listened.
Although you made a mistake that caused me pain.
As they always say," You never truly stray from the
first," So a place in my heart you will always
remain.

There was something different about you.
What we had was really special
I'm not sure what to call it
It had its own level
It became uncomfortable for him.
The strain that i placed.
I know it was stressful.
Precautions were made,
And they were successful.
I still miss our friendship.
I probably always will.

But at least the ride was zestful.

It all started so pure,
Before I removed your guard.
You skin was as smooth as silk
Before I left you scarred.
Although it was subconscious,
I still took advantage.
There was love for a good while, but it was difficult
to manage.
When you tried to counsel me,
I ignored your help.
I made huge mistakes. I gambled away our wealth
I know they've had a disastrous impact on your
overall health.
Even though I know by now you've forgiven me.
I'm still learning to forgive myself.

My life path equivalent.
For a while we were best friends.
We've known each other for so long,
You watched my journey begin
When I spilled my deepest sorrows
It was your ears I would depend
When I needed a place to cry,
Your shoulder you would lend.
Since we were so similar,
It was a natural blend.
We adored each other's company.

So much time we would spend.
By the time our love was romantic,
Our time was near it's end.
The love that you lost came back in your life.
From there you were forced to suspend.
Something so promising collapsed all of a sudden,
but I believe time will amend.
I have something to say to you, but I truly don't
wish to offend.
It'll sit on my tongue. If the timing strikes again,
I'll be sure to communicate it then.

Complete Freedom

Individuals in the world today have rights.
Although, some people may disagree
We have a place to live our lives,
But are we really completely free?

Are we free of diseases that take us away?
Free of the system that keeps us at bay.
Free of the lost ones that lead us astray.
Free of debt in which we have to repay.

Are we free of the fear that causes anxiety?
Free of children who weren't taught propriety.
Free of beings who dislike variety.
Free of pressures in our society.

Are we free of countries with a lack of food?
Free of the innocent being subdued.
Free of wars and unnecessary feuds.
Free of the truth they choose to exclude.

Are we free of the garbage that poisons our minds?
Free of situations that seem unkind.
Free of the lenses that turn our eyes blind.
Free of the habits that keep us behind.

Are we free of our loved ones getting abused?
Free of the populace being confused.
Free of the less fortunate getting accused.
Free of the privileged being excused.

I know mankind has come a long way.
I know we've grown exponentially.
But until we eliminate these plaguing issues,
We won't quite be completely free.

Unequilibrated

I don't know what's wrong with me.
I adjust my eyes, but I still can't see.
I don't understand, what could this be.
I've tried everything but it won't flee.

As soon as I get out of bed.
A sort of sickness which I dread.

The walls are still but they spin my head.
I'm forcibly lightened when I tread.

I've tried my hardest but can't ignore.
I'm rather annoyed, staying indoors.
An illness I've never experienced before.
What must I do to be restored?

My past spirit I'd like to scavenge.
My current posture I'm trying to salvage.
But please be careful I've lost my balance.
I hope to overcome this challenge.

My thoughts have become atrocious
I've developed a bit of psychosis.
I can't stand the accompanying neurosis
I require a professional diagnosis

Our Biggest Flaw

Where did this all begin?
My current level of awareness says, since we've
existed.
I'm not quite sure if that's the truth and I don't
think this content is listed.
In this place we occupy, who decides who is
assisted.
The overwhelming majority prioritize vicinity.

*In my interpretation, this factors into what makes
us twisted.*

I am no exception to the situation.
*I was once (and on occasion still am) open to what
you could call influenced ignorance*
We are born in the purest of light.
Impossible to preserve that innocence.
The current society we live in,
Excels at enabling us to be indifferent.
The level we've reached is unacceptable.
This is the problem most imminent.

*How can anyone see someone in pain, and not feel
a thing?*
*Why is it that some of us live like rodents, while
others live like queens and kings?*
*How can you call yourself humane, if you're too
preoccupied to see what we bring?*
*How can anyone feel happiness when our fellow
beings are suffering.*

*When I think about the reasoning, it leaves me in
disgust.*
*This is why it's exceedingly difficult, to find people
we trust.*
*Through history, those who rise in power, tend to
be unjust.*

I dislike the draining task of enlightening, but if I choose to live i must.

Pay close attention to every issue in the world.
It all boils down to one thing.
One, two, or a few individuals exercising their selfish ways.
Please listen carefully to these words.
Selfishness is the root of all evil.
It needs to be immediately purged
It's the only real problem to be solved.
Forget everything else you've heard.
The idea that you are more important than anyone else is absurd.
Whatever higher power you believe in, this is not what they preferred.
True selflessness is when you love everything that lives as much as you love yourself.
And that love can never be deterred.

Evolution

There's something about this picture that just don't seem right.
The sun is bright, but at night, the world has patches without light.
The structure in place is the furthest thing from airtight.
Surely, someone else has this insight.

There's something more we need to address.
We are unaware of the power we possess.
We've ignored the signals and signs of distress.
Even though you disagree, allow them to express
and don't think any less.

It was at this time, where the stars began to align.
Was there a mission in which each of us are
assigned?
Is there a map of sorts that each of us need to find?
Was mankind designed to live forever unrefined?
Is it undefined?
Who's the mastermind?
These thoughts put my mind in a bit of a bind. With
no way to unwind.

Right when I was about to flip my switch
It hit me.
We haven't yet evolved into what we need to be.
We haven't yet evolved to thinking unselfishly
We haven't yet evolved to agree to disagree.
We haven't yet evolved enough to see what we need
to see.

Now that I've come to this realization, what will I
do?
We won't reach this evolution before my life is
through.

There's one main goal I now must pursue.
One word at a time. I've got to breakthrough.
If I can change the view of a few.
We can build onto what's long overdue.

Infrequently Felt, Never Admitted

It may be for naught, but I'll stand my ground.
I struggle for the words that I feel
I've finally found the hidden treasure, but the
opening is locked.
I've yet to reach the thing that appeals.
That poker face is phenomenal.
I'm left guessing at the hand that you deal.
Impossible for me to solve this universally
challenging riddle when there's so much
information concealed.

I'm somewhat annoyed, but I'm also empathetic.
I know with caution you must proceed.
You recognize the fact that sometimes we are ill.
Many of whom move along, careful of the few who
pursue misdeeds.
In this realm, I assume you've experienced more
than most.
I'm sure there are thousands who'd beg and plead.
Forgive me as I envy the souls you acknowledge.
I am jealous of the ones who succeed.

Like water, I prefer to flow freely.
I'm never one that desires to impede.
You appreciate the purity that is the sunflower.
I imagine its drudgery sifting through the weeds.
The activities you handle with a bit of discretion.
I digress, but I am likely to heed.
Forgive me as I envy the souls you acknowledge.
I am jealous of the ones who succeed.

This space in which I dwell is pretty uncomfortable.
I rather dislike being in need.
I can't escape the black hole's pull.
Not even when moving at light-speed.
I know that jealousy is a deadly sin.
The wise say it's the cousin of greed.
Forgive me as I envy the souls you acknowledge.
I am jealous of the ones who succeed.

I grasp the importance of energy.
I'm aware if abused, it'll bleed.
The sincerest definition of the word anomaly.
The last of a dying breed.
A simplistically beautiful generational spirit
delighted for watering seeds.

I concede...

Forgive me as I envy the souls you acknowledge.

I am oh, so jealous of the ones who succeed.

Tell Me You Love Me

I'll work hard for you
Lay down my cards for you.
Let down my guard for you.
Leave my body scarred for you.
Do you love me now?

I'll give grace for you.
Paint my face for you.
Go to deep space for you.
Join the rat race for you.
Tell me you love me.

I'll dance for you.
Take a chance for you.
Take a stance for you.
Pay in advance for you.
Do you really love me now?

I'd go broke for you.
Tell jokes for you.
Remove my cloak for you
Inhale smoke for you.
Now tell me you love me.

I'll grow old for you.

Stay in the cold for you.
Change my goals for you.
Sell my soul for you.
Could you say that you love me now?

I would die for you.
Tell a lie for you.
Go awry for you.
So, before I cry, would you please,
Tell me you love me?

Tugging on My Discipline Strings

At the same time, both of my nostrils were sucker
punched.
Torture it is resisting those fumes.
I can still remember the taste.
I can still visualize it on my spoon.
It would behoove me to travel west.
I'll probably cave if I don't do it soon.
I've come too far now.
I won't surrender to which I no longer consume.

Sturdiness shaken; the pillars are breaking.
One foot through the door and my fate was sealed.
I've fought off the scent as much as I could, but
with your smile I could not deal.
Your mannerisms keep attracting my attention.
My productivity is what they kill.

The energy you exude is enchanting.
In proximity is where I'll be as I hope onto me, is where it spills.

Lowest of lows, the heaviest heads get.
Too proud to say I need a break.
I'm ashamed to admit I fell into a pit.
Some would call an egregious state.
Nortriptyline Played a role but never did it alleviate.
With scars to show, I fought that war.
No longer succumbing to capricious hate.

It's far too early for me to be awake.
I'd rather my position be replaced.
I struggle through grogginess to take my steps forward.
For what reason is that the case?
Chunks of the masses uphold an image.
It's exceedingly difficult to keep pace.
Signed and sealed, here's my resignation.
I'm done participating in this race.

Even though often detrimental.
The role you play is pivotal.
Who would I be without what makes me an individual?
Imagine if what circulated was deemed to be typical.

A world of my own creation.
Everything you could dream is mystical.
My loved ones can hardly see me as I've drifting
away.
It's about time that I alight toward the realm of the
physical.

Land of Love

Whisper in my ear as you glide along your way.
Rarely, have I been moved this way before.
Rejuvenate me while I sit and contemplate.
I feel as if I'm being soothed right down to my core.
Enriched, is what I feel in this state of being.
It's as simple as saying you are mine and I am
yours.
Foreign, the concept has been lately. I miss you
dearly.
How do I make them last forevermore?

Freer, I've never felt before this moment.
Susceptible to your loving embrace.
Peaceful, my mind and spirit have connected.
This purity can't be replaced.
Gleaming, the ray of sunshine is.
It's inscribed all over my smiling face.
Irrelevant, is the pain I felt today.
I let nothing influence this space.

Delightful, I feel, when there is light to be shined.
I'm busy most days so it's difficult to make time.
Energy in its purest form is unbelievably kind.
I'd had visions of you before.
What I brushed away then, I now take as a sign.
The passion exists and I am now keen.
To love I am much more inclined.

I've been your pupil a long time now.
My lenses have only recently started to clear.
I'll be learning from this point on.
I'll make an effort to enlighten the rest of my years.
Relieved, I feel for you've accepted me as I am.
I am incredibly grateful to be here.
Appreciative, I am, for this lovely opportunity.
As long as I exist on any plane, I guarantee I'll
hold you dear.

Greener Grass with Green Inside

It was time for a lifestyle change.
My health had reached an all-time low.
I had no idea of the damage I'd done.
Unaware of what I did and did not know.
Many benefits it's given me.
It enabled multiple areas of growth.
Almost ashamed it took me so long.
I should've seen it years ago.

When I decided to go plant based, I didn't think
this much would change
My body is as light as a feather.
Likely from its lessened overall strain.
My eyesight is a little less blurry.
I'm not legally blinded by rain.
My mentation reaches new heights.
My brain is in route to being what we call sane.

I never had a strong sense of smell.
Now I can smell the fresh air.
My stomach issues zapped my energy.
Now it feels as though it's perfect in there.
Sleep was always a struggle for my kind.
Now it brings no despair.
My spirit that had been broken for quite some time,
is slowly being repaired.

I sat around and wasting valuable days.
I could hardly move at all being that obese.
I don't hold negative energy nearly as long.
I recognize, learn, and then it's released.
I still fight through my injuries daily.
But the pain they cause has greatly decreased.
Even with chaos in my vicinity, through consistent
meditation, I can find peace.

*I don't usually deem it necessary to share in such
detail, but this I'll share with pride.
This Is my experience and in you I'll confide.
In my opinion, this is an early step toward us being
unified.
Our grass is greener when that green is inside.*

Jumper

*I hope you know I'm relentless in my pursuit.
I'm on your trail now that I've found a clue
The heat here is unbearable you couldn't have
settled.
I know I have much more to look through.
I've searched land with not much success.
Not many cleverer than you.
I'll buckle down from here on out.
I can't afford anymore miscues.*

*Jumped to space rock four and it's very different.
Everything here is brownish red.
I feel I'm on the right track.
I hope you remember what I said.
I can sense the fact the you were here and it's not
just games in my head.
The other individuals were easily fooled, but I'll be
much harder to shed.*

This time I'll jump to rock number 6.

I know your tendency is to skip the odds.
The atmosphere here is nothing short of amazing.
Those rings can only be an act of god.
I'm beginning to appreciate this effort of yours.
I'll use this moment to applaud.
I sprinted toward a trap as I thought I saw a face,
but alas, it was just a facade.

Rock 8 is here and I'm feeling lucky.
You can't be too far away now.
If I'm being honest, I'm getting a bit winded, but I
must finish what I vowed.
I see footsteps here, that's new for you.
I almost can't believe that you'd allow.
Through the jumps you taught me a lot.
At the very least that much, I'll avow.

I've found something. I think this it is.
Do I see what I think I see?
A plaque of information with everything I need.
Excuse me, while I try to contain my glee.
I walk up to it and it reads. "I didn't expect you be
so quick. I had to increase my speed. No one else
ever prevailed past this much debris. I've found a
way to jump to a new galaxy. Catch me if you can
on Proxima Centauri B."

A Message from Your Brother

I'll start with what's important.
I love you, even though is doesn't always show.
I'd like to clarify my current concerns, but I have a
feeling you already know.
I know you lose patience after waiting so long but
you have to take things slow.
I worry because I wish you nothing but good
health.
My sentiment expounded on below.

This society likes to create fairy tales.
For the most part it's not reality.
You seek security but it's elusive.
You think you've missed out and I agree.
Your fathers have failed in their parental duties.
There's no excuse in being absentee.
I wish I could go back in time.
Just maybe they'd hear my plea.

I can't imagine how tough it is.
I think you're incredibly strong.
I can't give you what you're searching for.
It's been inside you all along
We can't in this space though.
It's an unfortunate situation but life must go on.
We have to heal from our childhood trauma.
We have to try and right their wrongs.

I'll try my best to be there for you.

I'll try hard to play that role.
I'll try to fix the damage that's been done.
At least that's my overall goal.
Eventually you'll find someone suitable, but some
things are out of your control
No one can replace a father's love for you.
There is no one who could fill that whole.

As you look for someone to grow with.
I'll ask you to work on yourself.
If you aren't satisfied with what you have.
Be sure to work on your health.
I've found it's more about advancing the spirit.
Not all about acquiring wealth.
Not everyone has your interest at heart.
Exercise moving with stealth.

I don't speak to you enough, but I hope you gather
the messages I send.
I know you go through tough times.
Move forward until you reach the end.
The relationship should benefit both.
On yourself you should depend.
No being will be a picture of perfection.
True happiness can only come from within.

Worthiness

*I'm not sure if you're proud or not because I don't
know what you heard.
I try to paint pictures as much as I can. Let's hope I
find the right words.
As I maneuver around the only way I know how,
I'll conjugate the purpose I serve.
When I look back on what I've been given
throughout the years, I wonder what I really
deserve.*

*The love I have keeps me together.
At times I've taken it for granted.
The knowledge I've learned from impeccable
parents. Am I worthy of what they've implanted?
It was foolish of me to make that move,
I lose sense when I'm enchanted.
On the outside the path looks straight and narrow
but the roads I travel are slanted.*

*I speak from a place of concern, but I really have
no right to complain.
I wish I could untangle these cluttered thoughts but
It's really difficult to explain.
I've gathered some dirt lugging through the sand.
I cleanse by standing in the rain.
You can't fathom how much I regret what I've
done. I can't believe I caused so much pain.*

You tried to comprehend what I'm looking for.

It's the opposite of what you seek.
Through windows I seem like an oddball.
My ego says that I'm unique.
By now you think it would've faded, but you have
your mystique.
I've been climbing and climbing for years now.
Will I ever reach my mountain's peak?

Brain filled with questions galore.
Am I disciplined enough to run these miles?
Comfort me when I'm insecure.
Am I clever enough to make you smile?
I've held onto this energy for far too long.
Is it time for me to reconcile?
Have I done enough good to begin my ascension or
am I destined to burn for a while?

My Turn to Soar

This situation is potentially upsetting.
My recent desire had been to grow old.
I have yet to reach my full potential.
I did not quite heed the advice I was told.
I have yet to decipher through all the lies we've
been sold.
I'd planned on transforming your heart
into gold, but here on this fateful day,
my blood now runs cold.

*Although inconveniently timed, I'm not completely
surprised.
I've long had premonitions of an premature
demise.
If your face has dampened by this turn of events,
please dry your eyes.
There's no need to mourn a body my soul no longer
occupies.*

*My flesh has expired, but my spirit is alive and
well.
My energy surrounds you.
There is no need to bid farewell.
I only have one request. In this current space, do
not dwell.
There are far too many objectives in life that you
must quell.*

*If you ever harmed me in any way,
I didn't hold a grudge
I know the pain we hold inside at times becomes
too much.
Fight to master all your weaknesses.
Let nothing be your crutch.
Please use whatever skill or talent you were
awarded.
You never know who you can touch.*

I care for you deeply; I'll say it once more.

*I sincerely apologize if you've ever felt ignored
Forgive me for my shortcomings.
I'm an adventurer at my core.
My fascination to discover what's on the other side
of doors.*

*It's always been my destiny to learn from those that
came before.
I'm excited to have a whole new realm to explore.
Weep for a moment, then love forevermore.
The weights have been lifted.
And now, my friend, it's my turn to soar.*

<u>Short Stories</u>

Lonely House on The Lake

*"How did I get here? I was just on my home," I say
to myself. Now I'm in an area that doesn't look
familiar to me at all. "What do I do? " My phone is
dead and there is nothing around that can help me
in my navigation. I begin to walk in a random
direction. It's a grassy plains area with fair
weather so I guess it could be worse.*

*After a few hours of walking there I see a lovely
family home next to a sizable body of water. I make
my why way closer to what I can now tell is a lake
and there is a pale young girl dressed in all white
next to it. From about 50 feet away she realizes and*

runs up to me. Slightly out of breath she says, "Wow another person! I never see people around here. Will you come with me to my home? We have food." While I thought to myself it wasn't and ideal situation to be in, I accepted because I was starving. She escorts me to the family home and introduces me to her family members. They waste very little time speaking and go to the dinner table while offering me a seat. I can that they've laid out what looks like an entire feast, so I take my chair and sit quickly.

Halfway through the plate I was eating they all stop and gather around each other. They ask that I watch what they are about to do. To which I respond with a thumbs up because my mouth was full of food. They all slice their own foreheads and begin moving around the room, hissing as if they were snakes. I wanted to ask what in the world was going on, but I thought it was best to mind my own business. Especially since I was just about done with my food. "I'm going to leave now," I say with a very confused look on my face. The parents sigh and say, "You're about to miss the best part but ok." They point me in the direction of the nearest fire station so they could help me on my way home and make my way out. "Nice people but I hope I never see them again, "I say as I walk out of war shot range. They failed to mention it was many *miles away as well, so it ended being another few hours of walking. I eventually make it and they were kind enough to pay for my ticket I needed.*

Fast forward a couple of years. That experience had just about completely left my mind. I'm out on a random day taking a joy ride and my tire pops. I am disappointed in myself for being unprepared not having a spare. This time around my phone has charge but it's a dead zone with the signal so it's just as useless as before. Not too long after a stranger offers me a ride to the next town. I didn't see a problem with it, so I accepted. A little small talk here and there but I'm not really paying attention as I am focused on what I need to do to get back to my car and things. We come across a section in the road with terrible damage and detour signs begin to take us through dirt roads trying to connect to the other side of it. "We're coming up on a dangerous bridge," he says. I figured he was exaggerating so I wasn't too concerned. He ends up driving along this bridge that isn't very high over water. Not even a third of the way across, the bridge starts breaking apart. The vehicle begins to fall in. I conveniently see a canoe off to the side. It was very much a struggle to get to it as I'm a terrible swimmer. I look for the guy who was helping me but there was no sign of him at all. The waves in the water other than the ones I made. He just vanished. I paddle away as hard as I can to reach what looks like the closest edge of the river but the wind and current took the opposite way. It takes me through a few intersecting bodies of water before the current just stops completely. I look around a bit and something is familiar about it. "This is the same lake near that family from a few years ago." When it reaches the land area on the edge I was drifted to, I get out and see that same little girl from a couple of years before. "I see your back, she says loudly." She begins to speak some mystical craziness that just leaves me confused and at that moment I realize I must be connected to this place in some way, because of that ritual they did even though I didn't participate.

After she finished spewing madness, she told me if I wanted to know what was happening, I needed to follow her again back to the house. Me being the curious person I am I went along with it. There really wasn't much else to do being so far away from everything.

As soon as I take a step in the house I black out.

A wake up a little while later with a migraine and I'm finally enlightened to the situation at hand. My body is tied up over a stack of wood. I struggle to break free with all my might. The family is watching me from ten to fifteen feet away laughing and singing a song that sounds like it was made by demons. I begin to scream for help. The little girl

chuckles and says, "No one is coming here. You know no one is around here "
The rest of them rub their hands. This heat is becoming unbearable. I can no longer tell whether I'm sweating or not. I can hardly feel my limbs now. It seems like I won't make it out of this one. Right as I'm closing my eyes to accept my fate, a team of policemen make it to the scene. They were led to me by the guy I thought had drowned in the earlier accident. They made quick work arresting the entire family and putting out the fire that was burning me up. I thank them for what they had just done for me and they replied that they were just doing their jobs. I spent the next few months recovering in the hospital. I was thankful I survived with injuries that would eventually heal.
When I was finally healthy enough to leave, I made a promise to myself to never let that happen a second time. I told myself, "Don't you ever trust a little kid dressed in all white again. They aren't to be trusted."

Through These Eyes

A simple day on a stormy night in a foreign land. I decide to treat myself.
I walk in to partake in a hobby of mines.

"Let's see what I can find "I say out loud. There's a section for each of the main categories. Modern, Classic and Renaissance eras.

Newer things excite me so to the modern section I go. As I arrived so many vibrant colors catch my attention.

Then came the euphoric feeling I often feel when pursuing my passions. I scour the area trying to find what I feel is the best. Down to the last painting. It's isolated from the others almost as if it were in a completely different setting. I in my way overstep by step. By now I see an individual with a long trench coat on covering every inch of its body, still dripping from the storm outside. I reach the area and assume the individual is a woman. The lighting in the area is dull specifically for this piece. I see long, dark, curly hair protruding from the hood of the coat. I stand really close as I analyze the piece. There was something about it I couldn't place my finger on. I stare and stare at it for about 10 minutes before it finally hits me. I make a satisfied look on my face and she says," do you see it now". "Yes, I do. It took a while because this is unlike anything I've seen before but i think I've got it" I replied. "You have a keen eye. To most people this piece probably looks average. Only a select few can appreciate this one at its true value."

"Well thank you. What're you ——-"before I could finish my sentence she stops me and says, "I'm sorry, I've lost track of time I have somewhere I need to be at the moment". Disappointed I respond, "okay then" as she swiftly walks away. I sit there and think to myself as I do. "I wonder who she is". I return to enjoying the art in front of me for a while before I head back to my hotel. Before I knew it, I was asleep in bed and morning had come. I checked the time and realized "O I'm going to be late I should be leaving now"!! I quickly clean myself up, grab my things, check out of the hotel and head outside. I wave down a taxi. He stops in front. I get in and say, "To the airport, QUICKLY"!

He responds, "no problem, sir".

A few minutes go by and we've arrived. I pay the fare and run off. I race through security only to see that my watch was incorrect. There was still plenty of time before my flight was scheduled to depart. I decide to get a bite to eat at an exclusive restaurant on the inside. As I comb through the menu, I whisper to myself, "I should've followed her". I hear a tender voice behind me say, "you should've followed who?". I turn around and see a face that's unfamiliar but to the side the hair was identical. An eyebrow is raised. "Wait a second. You're the one from last night aren't you" I say smiling. "What?... what're you talking about?" She replies. "Oh, uhh, excuse me, I thought you were someone else" I say embarrassed. She smiled from ear to ear and says, "I'm joking. Yes, it was me. No one was supposed to recognize me. There you go showing off those eyes again". "Well if I'm gifted, I should put them to good use, right?" "You better" she quickly answers. Over the next few minutes, we engage in thought provoking, intellectual conversation. The euphoria returns but I notice something is off. Everyone around had begun to look at us out the corner of their eyes. As weird as it was, I didn't let in interrupt what was happening. A few people come up to us and ask "Who are you talking to? Are you ok, sir?" Slightly offended I respond, "I'm just fine and do you not see this person sitting across from me". They look at each other then back at me and say, "Uhh no we don't". I look across from me and I was floored. The woman had vanished and there was no sign of anyone having sat there. They walk away seemingly frightened. I place my hands on my head trying to process the situation. "What in the world is going on here." I think to myself. The waitress arrives with my food. "Here you go, sir. I hope you enjoy it". "Thank you very much", I respond to her. Ten minutes go by and I haven't even touched my food. I'm still racking my brain over what just happened. I finally decide to myself to eat and just figure it out later. I take a bite or two and feel I vibration in my pocket.

I've received a text from an unspecified number. At this point my confusion has been taken to an all-time high. Flabbergasted, I read the message. It reads, "I know what you're searching for. Our paths are intertwined. Until we meet again."